DOCTOR · WHO

MARTHA

BBC CHILDREN'S BOOKS
Published by the Penguin Group
Penguin Books Ltd, 80 Strand, London, WC2R 0RL, England
Penguin Group (USA), Inc., 375 Hudson Street, New York, New York 10014, USA
Penguin Books (Australia) Ltd, 250 Camberwell Road, Camberwell, Victoria 3124, Australia.
(A division of Pearson Australia Group Pty Ltd)
Canada, India, New Zealand, South Africa.
Published by BBC Children's Books, 2007
Text and design © Children's Character Books, 2007
Images © BBC 2004
Written by Moray Laing
Needle Point by Justin Richards.
10 9 8 7 6 5 4 3 2 1
Printed in China.
ISBN-13: 978-1-40590-309-7
ISBN-10: 1-40590-309-0

CONTENTS

Meet Martha

Introduction.................................4
Martha Data 6
Martha Anatomy...........................8
⬣ Test your knowledge

Friends and Family

The Doctor..............................10
Francine 11
Clive...................................11
Tish....................................12
Leo.....................................12
Adeola..................................13
⬣ Test your knowledge

Enemies and Rivals

The Judoon..............................14
The Plasmavore 14
The Carrionites.........................15
The Daleks..............................15
The Family of Blood.....................16
The Weeping Angels 16
The Master 17
⬣ Test your knowledge

No place like home

The Earth...............................18
Travels through time 20
⬣ Test your knowledge

Medical skills

Training................................22
Essential skills and Saving the World...22
Cardiopulmonary Resuscitation (CPR)......24
Concussion 25
⬣ Test your knowledge

Adventures at home...................26
⬣ Test your knowledge

Test your knowledge Answers 30

Needle Point.........................31

Like the rest of the Earth, medical student Martha Jones knew that aliens existed. She'd heard about a spaceship flying into Big Ben, she had witnessed the sinister Sycorax invasion and she lost a cousin during the horrific Battle of Canary Wharf. But what she didn't know was that one day she would meet the man who saved the world on those, and many more, occasions.

Martha met this man, the Doctor, while she was training to be a doctor herself at London's Royal Hope Hospital. Her life was safe and normal until then. She lived alone, she had exams coming up and she had a family that could, at times, go a bit mad.

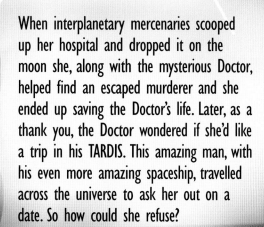

When interplanetary mercenaries scooped up her hospital and dropped it on the moon she, along with the mysterious Doctor, helped find an escaped murderer and she ended up saving the Doctor's life. Later, as a thank you, the Doctor wondered if she'd like a trip in his TARDIS. This amazing man, with his even more amazing spaceship, travelled across the universe to ask her out on a date. So how could she refuse?

Name: Martha Jones

Age: 23

Date of birth: 26 June 1983

Parents: Clive and Francine Jones

Sister: Tish Jones

Brother: Leo Jones

Height: 1.58m (5'2")

Hair: Black

Eyes: Brown

Home: London, England, UK, Earth

Species: Human

Profession: Medical student turned adventurer

1.58m tall

Martha can't believe what she's seeing half the time!

The Doctor makes her smile

Dressed for a night out with her family

Martha looks similar to her cousin Adeola

TEST YOUR KNOWLEDGE

THE DOCTOR

When Martha met the Doctor for the first time, she thought he was an ordinary patient in the hospital — until she listened to his pulse and realised he had two hearts! The Doctor was impressed by Martha's calm reaction and curiosity when the hospital was scooped on to the Moon by the Judoon. The Doctor had been travelling alone for some time, so at first he was unsure about taking Martha with him. He invited her along for one trip in the TARDIS, but it soon became a whole series of dangerous and exciting adventures!

FRANCINE

Francine Jones is Martha's mum. A professional
working woman, she has separated from
Martha's dad, Clive. She has a good
relationship with her three children,
but she finds Clive quite difficult.
At Leo's 21st birthday party, she
insulted Clive's girlfriend by
saying she looked orange. When
she saw Martha the next day
she thought her daughter was
slightly different but couldn't work
out why. And when she met the Doctor
she had a feeling that his friendship with
Martha could be dangerous!

CLIVE

Martha's dad, Clive Jones, is a successful
and wealthy businessman. However, he
does seem to be having a bit of a mid-
life crisis. He drives a flashy sports car
and his girlfriend, Annalise, is about the
same age as Martha. He's a good dad,
though, and his children all love him.

TISH

Tish, short for Letita, is slightly older than Martha and relies on her to keep the peace between her argumentative family! When Martha and the hospital disappeared into thin air she really panicked. Tish worked for a short time as a senior PR assistant for Professor Lazarus. Although she's close to Martha, she's cross that every time she meets someone, Martha finds fault. She thinks the Doctor is a science geek, but she is probably a bit jealous of Martha's exciting new friend.

LEO

Leo is the youngest of the Jones family. He lives with his girlfriend, Shonara, and they have a baby, Keisha. His 21st birthday brought his whole family together - but soon pushed them all apart! After his dad's girlfriend stormed out of his party, the family all went home arguing - except Martha, who disappeared in time and space.... .

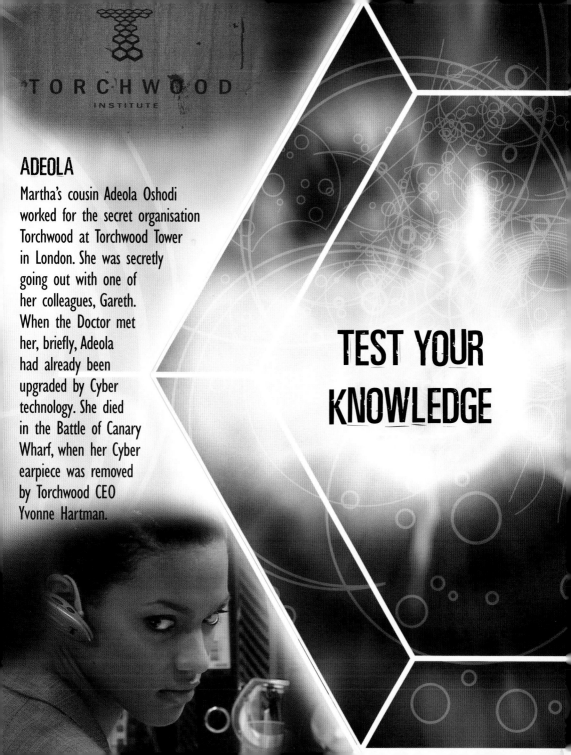

TORCHWOOD
INSTITUTE

ADEOLA

Martha's cousin Adeola Oshodi worked for the secret organisation Torchwood at Torchwood Tower in London. She was secretly going out with one of her colleagues, Gareth. When the Doctor met her, briefly, Adeola had already been upgraded by Cyber technology. She died in the Battle of Canary Wharf, when her Cyber earpiece was removed by Torchwood CEO Yvonne Hartman.

TEST YOUR KNOWLEDGE

THE JUDOON

The Judoon were the first aliens Martha came face to face with. The brutish Judoon are a troop of space police in leather kilts and hefty boots. These interplanetary thugs were looking for an escaped Plasmavore, and they picked up Martha's hospital and everyone in it with an H_2O scoop. They placed it on to the neutral territory of the Moon when they thought they had found the missing alien.

THE PLASMAVORE

The sinister Florence Finnegan may look like an old lady in her seventies, but she is actually an escaped alien called a Plasmavore. She murdered the Child Princess of Padrivole Regency Nine and was hiding in a London hospital when Martha met her. A hospital, with all its blood banks, was the perfect place for a Plasmavore as they need blood to survive. She used a bendy straw to drain blood from her victims and had two slave drones called Slabs to help her.

THE CARRIONITES

The Carrionites disappeared back at the dawn of the universe, banished into the Deep Darkness by the Eternals. Nobody knew if they were ever real or just a legend. They use shapes and words as power. When the Doctor and Martha arrived in London in 1599 they discovered that three Carrionites had managed to escape and, using the words of William Shakespeare, were about to free the rest of their race. Martha gave Shakespeare a new word from the Harry Potter novels to say, which expelled them from our world: 'Expelliarmus!'

THE DALEKS

The Daleks are one of the most evil races in the whole universe. But there aren't many left now. Four special Daleks, the Cult of Skaro, ended up in 1930s New York and continued with their mission to find new ways of killing enemies and staying alive. The Daleks stole more than a thousand humans and wiped their minds — ready to fill them with Dalek ideas and create a Human Dalek race.

THE FAMILY OF BLOOD

The Family of Blood are a nasty race of hunters with an amazing ability to sniff out anyone they want. When the Family's lifespans were running out they wanted the Doctor. They tracked him down across time and space, so the Doctor became human and then hid with Martha in a school in 1913 and waited for them to die. The Family of Blood travelled far and wide looking for him and eventually ended up at the school. By using molecular fringe animation to create animated scarecrows and taking over the bodies of some humans they managed to find the Doctor.

THE WEEPING ANGELS

The Weeping Angels look like ancient stone statues. They used to be known as the Lonely Assassins and no one knows where they come from. Thankfully, the Weeping Angels kill you quite nicely — as the Doctor and Martha found out. They simply zap you into the past and let you live out your lifespan until you die in your own past.

THE MASTER

The Master is a Time Lord like the Doctor. But unlike the Doctor he is after power and glory. Pretending to be Harold Saxon, the Master became Prime Minister of Britain and then took over the world, enslaving the human race. Martha spent a whole year travelling round the world finding a way to defeat the Master…

TEST YOUR KNOWLEDGE

THE EARTH

Martha comes from the planet Earth, the third planet from the sun. Its one satellite, the Moon, was visited by Captain Neil Armstrong in 1969 and Martha's visited it too! She found herself there thanks to the Judoon. According to Galactic Law, the Judoon have got no jurisdiction over the Earth, so they isolated a bit of the planet with an H_2O scoop and conducted their thuggish investigation from the Moon.

While everyone around her was screaming and afraid, Martha looked out in wonder at the Moon's surface and thought it was beautiful. In the distance she could see her home planet.

Home was a flat in London, although, when she started travelling with the Doctor, home became a blue police box called the TARDIS, which was bigger on the inside than the outside. The Doctor's TARDIS is an incredible spaceship that can travel anywhere in time and space. On her first trip, Martha wondered if the Doctor needed to pass a test to fly it and wanted to know what makes it travel in time. The Doctor refused to explain though, preferring to keep the mystery of his marvellous machine!

TRAVELS THROUGH TIME

Martha's first experience of time travel took her to her hometown of London — 400 years before she was born. She worried that she might change time by just being there, but with the help of the Doctor she soon got used to the idea of walking around in the past. While there she met the famous writer William Shakespeare, who really fancied her!

But one trip in time was not enough, so the Doctor took Martha into the far future. They landed in the year five billion and fifty-three — planet New Earth, the second home of mankind — fifty thousand light years away from Martha's home.

Later, Martha found herself stuck in history on a couple of occasions. To hide from aliens, she spent two months in Farringham School for Boys in Hereford in 1913, the year before the First World War. She became a maid in the school and was left to look after a human version of the Doctor. She didn't like the way women were treated back then.

Another time, she and the Doctor were thrown back into the past when they encountered a Weeping Angel. They found themselves trapped in 1969 and Martha had to get a job in a shop and support the Doctor while he worked out a clever way of getting the TARDIS back.

TEST YOUR KNOWLEDGE

Wherever, or whenever, they go, Martha is always amazed at what she sees. No two days are the same. Not many people get the chance to travel with the Doctor. She realises how lucky she is and loves every minute of it. But when they finally managed to defeat the Master, Martha had a very difficult decision to make. Should she stay at home with her family, or keep travelling with the Doctor?

TRAINING

Martha Jones was a medical student training at the Royal Hope Hospital in London. Doctors have to train for several years. It's not an easy profession and to succeed as a doctor, students, like Martha, have to work incredibly hard and pass many exams.

Martha is nearing the end of her training - and the skills she has learned as a student come in very handy while she's travelling with the Doctor.

ESSENTIAL SKILLS

Martha has got the perfect character for being a doctor. She cares about people and always wants to help where she can. She is able to keep calm when others are panicking. While stuck on the Moon she continued to reassure patients that everything would be all right. She even promised the Doctor that she would get him back to Earth!

Not everyone she has met believes she could be a doctor. She had to prove she was training to be a doctor to a nurse Joan Redfern in 1913, so she described all the bones in the hand.

SAVING THE WORLD

With the Doctor and Captain Jack both held prisoner by the Master on his flying aircraft carrier, Valiant, it was up to Martha to save the world. She spent a year organising people and bringing them hope - and a way of defeating the Master once and for all.

CARDIOPULMONARY RESUSCITATION (CPR)

On many occasions Martha has had to use cardiopulmonary resuscitation (known as CPR) to help people breathe when they have fallen unconscious. This involves chest compressions and giving some of your own breath into a patient's lungs.

On the Moon, after the Doctor had been attacked by the Plasmavore, Martha did everything she could to save the Doctor. While oxygen was running out in the hospital, she gave her last bit of air to revive him.

In London, 1599, she tried to save Lynley when he was drowned by witchcraft. She later rescued the Doctor from a Carrionite attack by thumping his heart.

When Captain Jack Harkness was electrocuted she tried to revive him too — but thanks to his immortality, he managed to come back to life by himself.

CONCUSSION

Concussion is caused by an injury to the head and can be extremely serious. Martha is always quick to check people for it. When her brother Leo bumped his head, she got her mum to put an improvised ice pack on Leo's head and hold it down to reduce the swelling. And while the Doctor was stuck in a human body, he fell down some stairs and Martha was keen to know if the Matron had checked him for concussion.

TEST YOUR KNOWLEDGE

An ordinary day for Martha Jones turned into the most fantastic day of her life! In the Royal Hope Hospital everything was normal until rain started raining upwards and the entire hospital was kidnapped and transported to the Moon! Martha realised something was strange when she discovered she could still breathe and decided to trust the man who had checked into the hospital earlier that day. This man, the Doctor, later offered her one trip in his TARDIS.

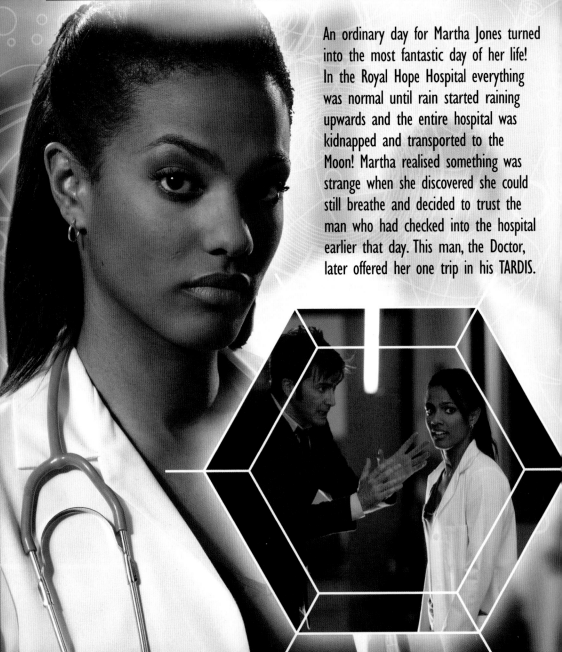

Of course, one trip in the TARDIS is never enough! Martha went to the past twice and the far future before the TARDIS took her home. She arrived back on the morning after she had left, yet in that time Martha had met aliens, saved the world, and nearly kissed Shakespeare! While back home, she and the Doctor ended up going to a party for Professor Lazarus' new machine. Dormant genes in Lazarus's DNA reactivated something that evolution rejected millions of years ago and awoke a horrible creature. After this, Martha became a full-time traveller with the Doctor.

When the TARDIS arrived in Wester Drumlins House in present day Earth, it wasn't long before ancient creatures called Weeping Angels attacked the Doctor and Martha. The time travellers found themselves trapped in the past — in a time long before Martha was born!

Martha and the Doctor paid a short visit to present-day Cardiff to get fuel for the TARDIS. Cardiff is built on a rift in the space/time continuum — which provides perfect energy for the Doctor's ship. When they left Cardiff, the TARDIS ended up going further into time and space than ever before. And, on the outside of the TARDIS, an old friend of the Doctor's, Captain Jack Harkness, was travelling with them.

When they returned to London, it was to find that the Doctor's oldest enemy — the Master — was now in charge. Hunted by the security services, Martha was about to start the most dangerous and exciting adventure of her life...

TEST YOUR KNOWLEDGE

ANSWERS

Meet Martha
1 (c) 2 (b) 3 (a) 4 (c) 5 (c)

Friends and Family
1 (a) 2 (c) 3 (b) 4 (c) 5 (b)

Enemies and Rivals
1 (b) 2 (c) 3 (a) 4 (c) 5 (b)

No place like home
1 (b) 2 (c) 3 (a) 4 (c) 5 (b)

Medical skills
1 (b) 2 (a) 3 (a) 4 (b) 5 (c)

Adventures at home
1 (a) 2 (c) 3 (b) 4 (c) 5 (a)

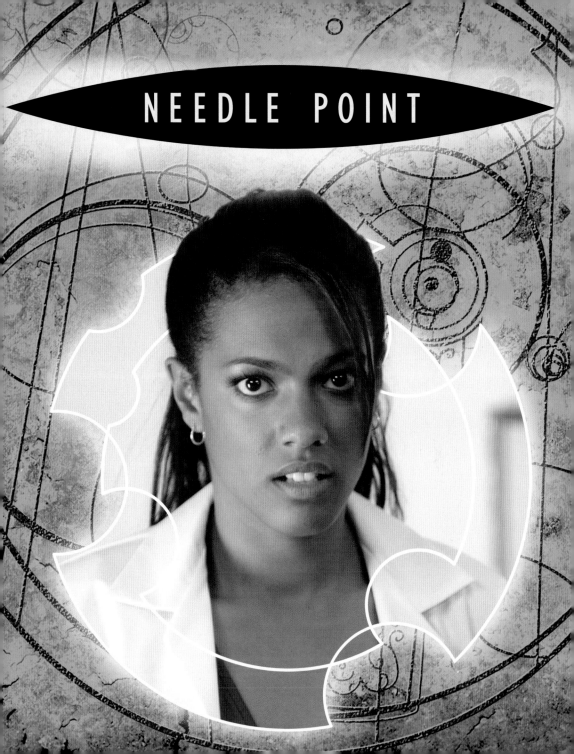

NEEDLE POINT

When they walked past the coffee bar for the third time, Martha decided that enough was enough. She stopped and folded her arms.

The Doctor, examining the small gadget he was carrying, didn't notice and kept walking. After about ten metres, he paused and glanced up. Catching sight of Martha, he grinned and waved the gadget at her. It was about the size of a mobile phone, with a dial on the top and a little stubby aerial sticking out.

'That's the third time we've walked along here,' Martha told him, without moving. She let the Doctor walk back to her.

'Oh, I should think so,' he said. 'Definitely an etheric beam somewhere round here.' He held the box up and turned slowly in a circle. 'Bit muffled, that's why the signal's weak. But etheric. And alien.'

'Dangerous?' Martha asked.

'Well… Maybe a six, seven perhaps on the Danger Scale.'

'Out of how many? Ten? I mean are we talking end of the world or a storm in a coffee cup?' The smell from the coffee bar was rich and inviting.

'Probably just a stranded alien gathering etheric energy to power up his ship,' the Doctor said. 'Or,' he admitted, 'it might be

some purely natural blip. Might be a double-decker that needs its engine tuning.'

There was a double-decker bus just turning off the street further along. Martha did not fancy running after it. In fact, the more she smelled the coffee, the more that was what she fancied. She sat down at one of the small round tables on the pavement.

'How about I leave you to it, and you can tell me whether it was Albert Alien or Derrick Double Decker when you're done?'

'Oh it won't take long,' the Doctor insisted. 'Two shakes.' To prove it he shook the gadget. Twice. Then he frowned at it. 'That can't be right. Tell you what, why don't you wait here and I'll be back when I'm done. It's a nice day, so you just chill.'

There wasn't much chance of that, Martha thought as she ordered coffee and a cake. It was a beautiful summer's day and she moved her chair slightly to bring it into the shade. The town centre was washed with sunlight. She watched the people walking past – a

man with a small dog, a woman pushing a pram, an elderly lady, a man and a woman holding hands but arguing, another old lady walking the other way...

Or, hang on, it was the same old lady. Martha recognised the hesitant slightly stiff walk, the way she was a little stooped. The grey-white hair arranged and pinned up, the shapeless brown cardigan and black handbag. Martha smiled at the lady and sipped her coffee. The lady ignored her and continued on her way.

After a few minutes the Doctor returned. He was on the other side of the road, still staring at the dial on the gadget. Martha waved, but he didn't see her. In fact, he was so intent on the dial that he didn't even see the person walking towards him and almost bumped into her.

Martha laughed out loud as she saw the Doctor's apologetic gestures and the glare of the old lady he'd almost knocked off the pavement. The old lady was wearing a shapeless brown cardigan and carrying a black handbag.

DOCTOR·WHO

The same little old lady. Again.

But – she had just passed by heading in the other direction. There was no way the old lady could have got round the block and back on the other side of the road in that time. Not unless she was an Olympic sprinter. Martha stared at the old lady walking hesitantly along again. She was obviously not an Olympic sprinter. How odd…

By the time she had seen the old lady several times more, Martha was beyond thinking it

was odd. The same old lady went into a shop further along the street. Then she came out of a different shop. Now she was crossing the road at the other end. And coming out of the first shop again. What was going on?

There was no sign of the Doctor, so Martha left the money for her coffee and cake and waited for the old lady to pass by yet again. She did not have to wait long. She let the lady get a few metres ahead, then followed. Did the old lady have a teleport, or some ability to zap through space in a moment? There was no sign of it as the old lady went into a shop.

It was an antiques shop, and Martha could see the old lady walking slowly to the back. Martha waited a moment, then followed her inside. The shop was dusty, run-down, and full of what Martha considered to be junk rather than antiques. There were piles of old books, broken bits of furniture and a sofa that was so faded you couldn't tell what colour it used to be.

There was no sign of anyone, so Martha made her way through the shop, following the old lady. At the back of the shop was a door, standing slightly open. Martha could hear something from the other side, and peered carefully round.

The door opened into a large back room. There were several armchairs and a sofa, all in as sorry a condition as the furniture in the shop. Upright chairs were arranged round the walls. But it wasn't the furniture that made Martha's eyes widen in surprise. The room was full

of old ladies. There must be about twenty of them – sitting, standing, talking quietly, and knitting. All of them knitting, with big chunky needles.

But two things made Martha's heart thump in her chest. First, although the old ladies were knitting, none of them had any wool. And when she looked closely, Martha saw that the needles never touched, just danced round each other in a complicated repeating pattern.

The second thing – the one that really got Martha – was that all the old ladies were the same. Exactly the same. She was seeing the exact same old lady, but about twenty times.

Time to get the Doctor, Martha decided. She turned slowly, quietly away from the door. And found yet another identical old lady standing right behind her. This old lady was holding what looked like a toy space gun. But the way she held it suggested to Martha that it wasn't really a toy and the person holding it wasn't really an old lady.

'Inside, human spy,' the old lady said in a cracked, failing voice.

'Look what I found outside, spying on us,' she said as she and Martha stepped into the room.

The old ladies inside went on 'knitting'. 'We'll have to kill her, of course,' one of them said, in the same cracked voice.

'If we can spare the power,' another added.

'Levels are building, but we are still very short of etheric energy,' another said.

'You're aliens,' Martha said, trying to sound like she wasn't at all bothered. 'Aliens disguised as little old ladies.' Despite the gun jabbing into her back, she couldn't help asking: 'What's that all about? And what do you think you're knitting?'

The old lady with the gun cackled a laugh. 'Knitting? We are gathering energy with the etheric antennae. When we have stored enough power we shall make our report to the fleet commander.'

'And what will you report? That shapeless brown cardies are the in fashion here on Earth?'

One of the old ladies jabbed a knitting needle at Martha. 'Silence, human! Do not let our frail appearance confuse you. We are short of energy, that is why we are gathering more.' She returned to knitting furiously. 'When we arrived, we had only enough power to create one disguise pattern.'

'So that's why you all look the same,' Martha realised. 'But why do you look like that? Wouldn't be my first choice, I can tell you.'

'Then you are stupid,' the lady with the gun said. 'Our analysis of human observational behaviour indicated this was the best pattern. As far as humans are concerned, all little old ladies look the same. So you fail to notice twenty identical disguised aliens in the same small area.'

'And you will all pay for that mistake when the fleet arrives,' another of the ladies said. The ladies slowly stood up, advancing menacingly on Martha, knitting needles whirling in front of them.

'All except you,' the old lady with the gun told Martha. 'Because you will already be – '

But she got no further, because Martha turned suddenly and knocked the gun aside. A bolt of blue lightning shot across the room and slammed into the wall. Martha grabbed the gun and tried to wrench it free of the old lady's grasp.

'Energy discharge,' one of the ladies hissed. 'Do not waste the energy. If we don't report, the fleet will move on and abandon this planet.'

'Sounds good to me,' Martha said. She managed to pull

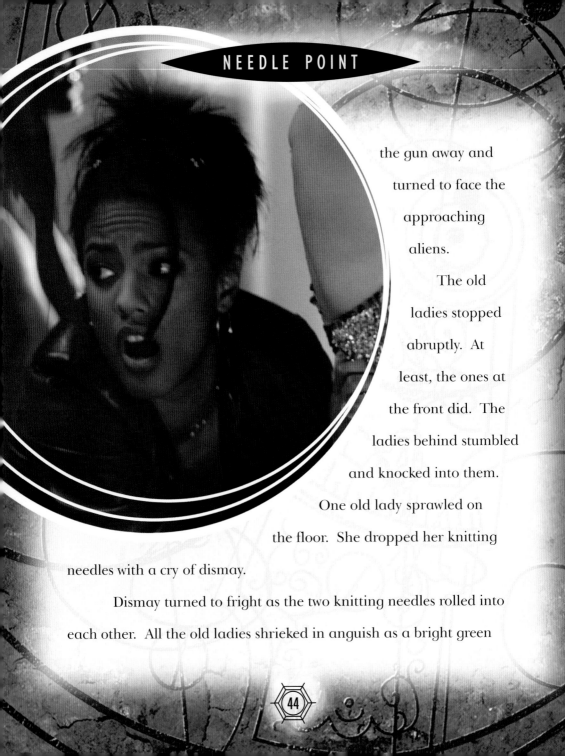

the gun away and turned to face the approaching aliens.

The old ladies stopped abruptly. At least, the ones at the front did. The ladies behind stumbled and knocked into them. One old lady sprawled on the floor. She dropped her knitting needles with a cry of dismay.

Dismay turned to fright as the two knitting needles rolled into each other. All the old ladies shrieked in anguish as a bright green glow suddenly surrounded the needles.

Martha backed slowly away. The ladies seemed to be ignoring her now. The green light was spreading – and all the knitting needles were glowing.

'We are losing energy!' one of the ladies shrieked. But her voice was no longer an old lady's. It was deeper, more of a growl. And the lady's face was a shining green and seemed to be melting. All the old ladies were glowing and changing as Martha watched.

It was hard to see through the intense green light, but they looked more like huge grasshoppers than old ladies now. Spindly front legs waved desperately in the air. Huge segmented eyes stared angrily at Martha.

Then the glow faded, and when it had gone, so had the aliens. No old ladies, no giant grasshoppers, no knitting needles, and no space gun.

Outside the shop, the Doctor was tapping at the dial on his

gadget. He looked up as Martha stepped out into the bright sunshine beside him.

'Ah, there you are,' he said. 'Thought I'd traced the etheric energy, but now it seems to have gone.' He shook the gadget. 'No – nothing. Must have been a blip. Or a bloop. Or maybe a blarb, you never know.' He stuffed the gadget into his coat pocket and grinned at Martha. 'Never mind. You been having fun?'

'Well, sort of,' she said. She wasn't sure where to start.

But the Doctor was already walking away, hands thrust deep into his coat pockets. He paused outside the next shop.

There was a pram outside on the pavement. Martha remembered watching a young woman push it past the coffee bar. By the time she caught up with the Doctor, he was grinning at the baby lying in the pram and making coochy-coo noises at it. The baby stared back at him, unimpressed.

'Mum must have nipped into the shop,' Martha said. She smiled at the baby too – amused by its blue eyes and bald head. It was tiny. But at least it would grow up without its planet being invaded by giant grasshoppers.

'Come on then,' the Doctor decided, nudging Martha's shoulder with his own. He still had his hands in is coat pockets. 'You know,' he said as they walked past another woman pushing another pram, 'it's funny how all babies look the same, isn't it?'